Climb every mountain, bounce every check...

A CATHY® SUNDAY COLLECTION

by Cathy Guisewite

Andrews and McMeel, Inc.
A Universal Press Syndicate Company
Kansas City • New York

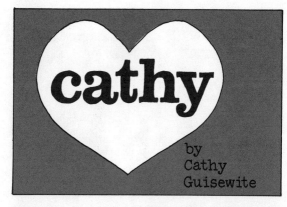

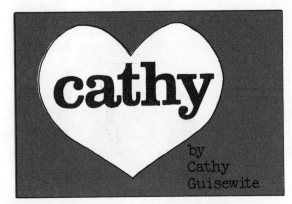

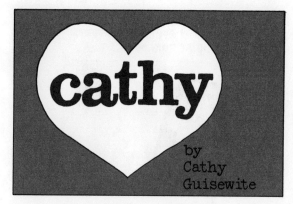

by
Cathy
Guisewite

I SPENT THE ENTIRE DAY ON MY EXPENSE REPORTS.

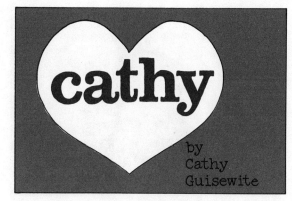

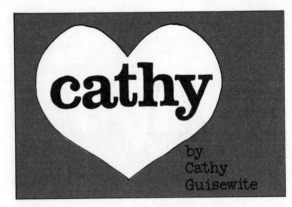

cathy

by Cathy Guisewite

GO FOR IT.

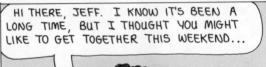
HI THERE, JEFF. I KNOW IT'S BEEN A LONG TIME, BUT I THOUGHT YOU MIGHT LIKE TO GET TOGETHER THIS WEEKEND...

REMEMBER ME ? I'M CATHY. CATHY, WITH THE LONG, SILKY HAIR...

CATHY, WITH THE DEEP, BROWN EYES...

CATHY, WITH THE WARM WIT... THE SWEET, SENSITIVE SMILE....

CATHY, WITH THE INCOME TAX RETURNS SHE HASN'T EVEN STARTED WORKING ON YET ??...

CPA'S ARE A TOUGH BREED.

Guisewite 4·12

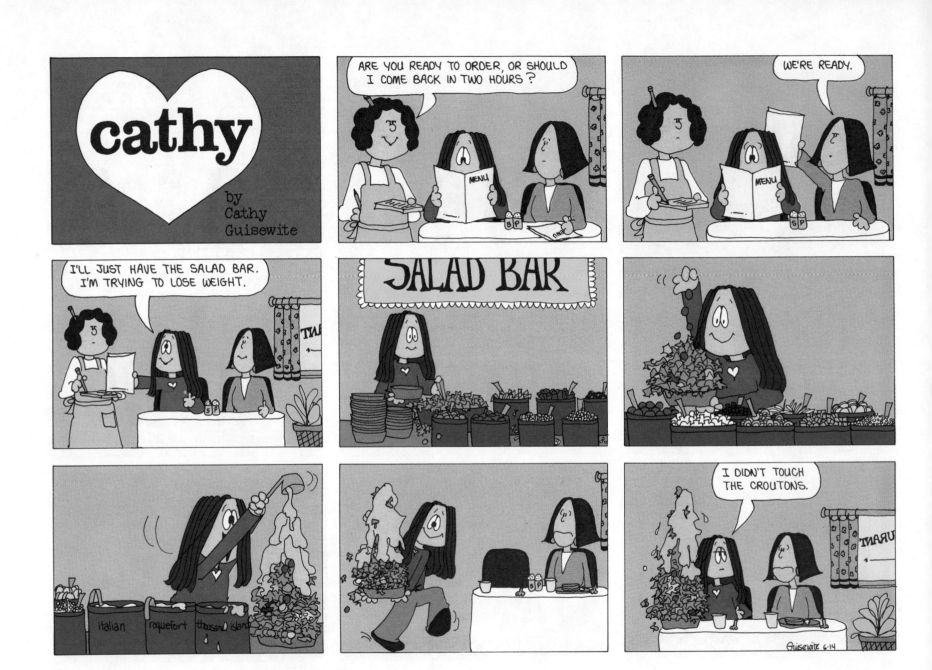

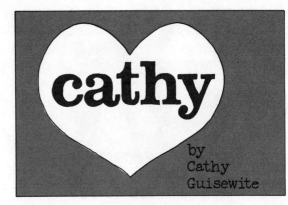

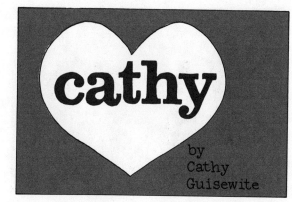

cathy

by Cathy Guisewite

THUNDER THUNDER

THE POOL! GRAB YOUR BACKGAMMON SETS, ICE UP YOUR COOLERS AND LET'S **ALL HIT THE POOL**!!

VOLLEYBALL! **COME ON, EVERYONE!** TO THE COURTS FOR VOLLEYBALL!!

YAHOO! **BARBEQUE**!! FIRE UP THOSE COALS AND LET'S CHOW DOWN!!

HEY, HEY! IT'S GROUP CAR WASH TIME! YEAH!! PUT ON THE GRUBBIES AND HOSE DOWN THE MACHINES!!!

THE POOL!! YEEHAH!! EVERYONE BACK TO THE POOL!!

WHY DON'T YOU EVER MEET ANYONE IN YOUR OWN APARTMENT BUILDING, CATHY?

I CAN'T CHANGE CLOTHES FAST ENOUGH.

Guisewite 7-19

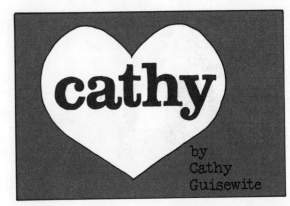

I WONDER IF I'LL MARRY THIS MAN.

I ONLY MET HIM 20 MINUTES AGO, BUT YOU NEVER KNOW...

I WONDER WHAT HE'LL BE LIKE WHEN HE'S 60. I WONDER IF HE'LL BE HAPPY AND SUCCESSFUL OR FRUSTRATED AND CRANKY...

I WONDER IF HE'LL GET BALD AND FAT AND BORING... I WONDER IF HE'LL...

THIS IS TERRIBLE. I'M SPENDING ALL THIS TIME PROJECTING INTO THE FUTURE, AND POOR RON IS SITTING THERE THINKING I'M JUST IGNORING HIM.

WHAT WERE YOU SAYING, RON?

I WONDER IF SHE'LL GET GREY AND FLABBY...

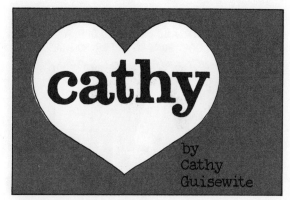

cathy

by Cathy Guisewite

HAVEN'T WE BEEN THROUGH ENOUGH WEDDINGS THIS WEEK WITHOUT THIS ONE, ANDREA?

IT WAS VERY IMPORTANT TO NAOMI THAT WE COME, CATHY.

WHERE **IS** NAOMI?

THERE... SOBBING INTO THE NATURAL FIBER HANDKERCHIEF...

IT WAS A VERY NICE WEDDING, NAOMI.

IT WAS WHAT MY DAUGHTER WANTED.

I ALWAYS DREAMED SHE'D GET MARRIED IN AN ORGANIC VEGETABLE GARDEN LIKE I DID... ..BUT NO, LOTUS HAS A MIND OF HER OWN.

I SAID, "SWEETIE, THE GROOM COULD WEAR AN AMERICAN FLAG AND BRAID HIS HAIR WITH WILD FLOWERS JUST LIKE YOUR DADDY DID... ...I WILL BAKE CARROT CAKE AND MACRAME A VEIL!"

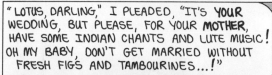

"LOTUS, DARLING," I PLEADED, "IT'S **YOUR** WEDDING, BUT PLEASE, FOR YOUR **MOTHER**, HAVE SOME INDIAN CHANTS AND LUTE MUSIC! OH MY BABY, DON'T GET MARRIED WITHOUT FRESH FIGS AND TAMBOURINES...!"

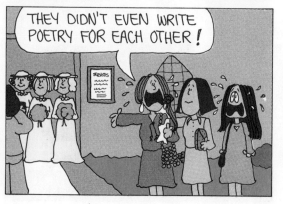

THEY DIDN'T EVEN WRITE POETRY FOR EACH OTHER!

WHAT ARE **YOU** CRYING FOR, CATHY??

I DON'T KNOW WHICH GENERATION GAP I BELONG TO.

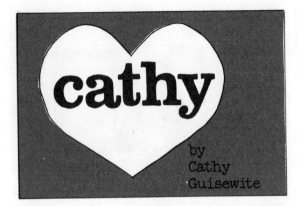

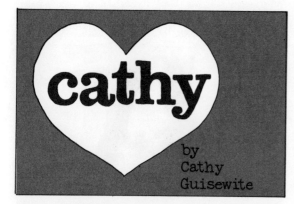

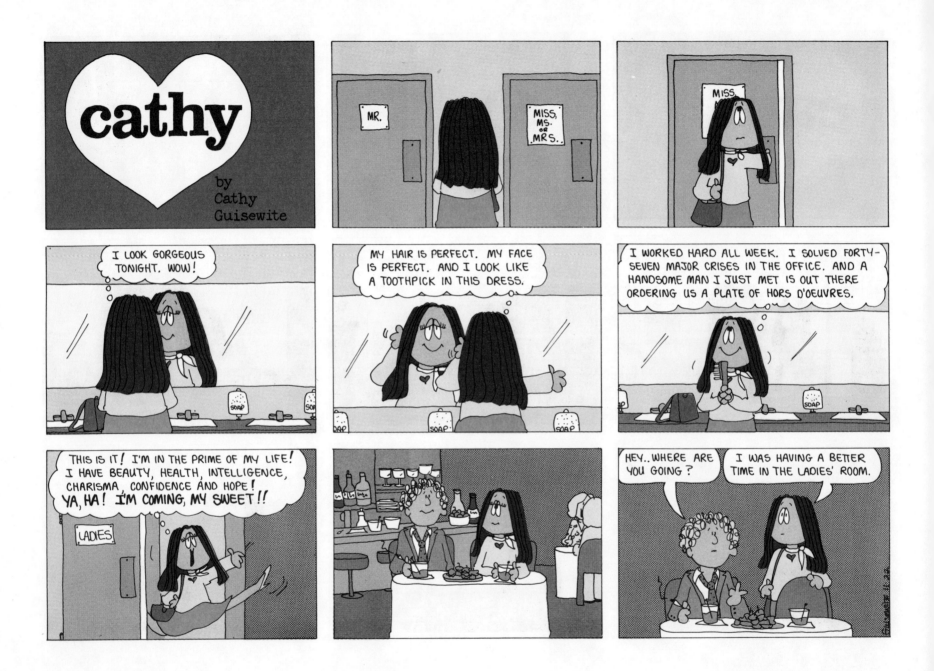

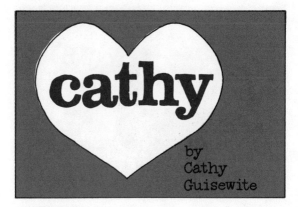

cathy

by Cathy Guisewite

WHERE DO YOU WANT ME TO PUT THESE, CATHY?

THROW THEM ON THE FLOOR WITH EVERYTHING ELSE.

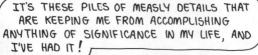

LOOK AT THIS PIT, MOM. PILES OF PAPERWORK FROM THE OFFICE... PILES OF DIRTY CLOTHES ... PILES OF THINGS TO FIX...

IT'S THESE PILES OF MEASLY DETAILS THAT ARE KEEPING ME FROM ACCOMPLISHING ANYTHING OF SIGNIFICANCE IN MY LIFE, AND I'VE HAD IT!

MY LIFE IS TICKING AWAY, AND I'M USING IT UP ON TRIVIAL PROJECTS THAT WON'T MAKE ONE SPECK OF DIFFERENCE IN THE LONG RUN.

I **KNOW** I CAN DO MORE THAN THIS, MOM! LOOK AT ME!!!

ALL DRIVE, NO DIRECTION.

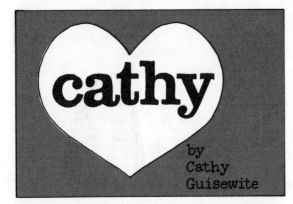

WELL, I'D BETTER GET GOING, CATHY.

OKAY,.. SEE YOU SOON, IRVING.

HI, IT'S ANDREA. DID YOU FINALLY HAVE THAT TALK WITH IRVING?

THERE JUST WASN'T TIME, ANDREA.

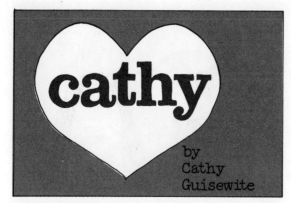

cathy

by
Cathy
Guisewite

IF THE PHONE RINGS, I'M NOT GOING TO ANSWER IT. I HAVE TOO MUCH WORK TO DO TODAY.

OKAY. MAYBE I'LL ANSWER IT... BUT I'LL SAY, "I'M SORRY, I'M BUSY. I'LL HAVE TO CALL YOU BACK."

OKAY. MAYBE I'LL ALLOW ONE SHORT CONVERSATION, BUT THAT'S IT! POSITIVELY NO MORE CALLERS!!

DIAL DIAL DIAL DIAL

HI, MOM. WHAT'S NEW?

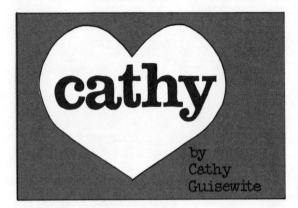

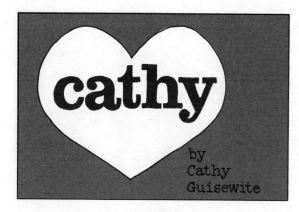

by
Cathy
Guisewite

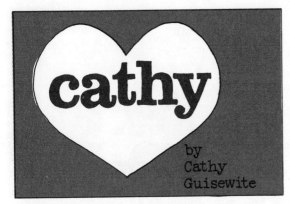

cathy

by Cathy Guisewite

MY LIST IS GETTING LONGER.

I KNOW WHAT YOU MEAN.

MY LIFE IS GETTING SHORTER AND MY LIST IS GETTING LONGER...

AT FIRST, ALL I WAS LOOKING FOR WAS INTELLIGENCE AND A SENSE OF HUMOR.

YEAH... INTELLIGENCE, HUMOR AND TAN SUITS. HE HAS TO WEAR TAN SUITS AND SKINNY TIES.

AND BE SHORT. A SHORT, BRIGHT, WITTY MAN WHO WEARS TAN SUITS AND SKINNY TIES AND KNOWS HOW TO COOK.

DON'T FORGET THE PIANO. HE MUST PLAY THE PIANO, AND HAVE A LAW DEGREE AND BURGUNDY FURNITURE, AND HE NEVER THROWS HIS TOWELS ON THE FLOOR. ALSO, HE LOVES TO GARDEN.

YES! BUT HE GAVE UP HIS LAW PRACTICE TO BECOME A VETERINARIAN. A SHORT VEGETARIAN VETERINARIAN WHO PLAYS THE PIANO WEARING TAN SUITS AND SKINNY TIES AND COOKS CANDLELIGHT JAPANESE MEALS WHICH HE SERVES IN THE BURGUNDY LIVING ROOM OF HIS METICULOUS STEAMBOAT SPRINGS TOWNHOUSE WHICH HE BUILT BY...

MARILYN, WAIT... LOOK OVER THERE!

I ONLY DATE REDHEADS.

MEN HAVE GOTTEN SO PICKY.

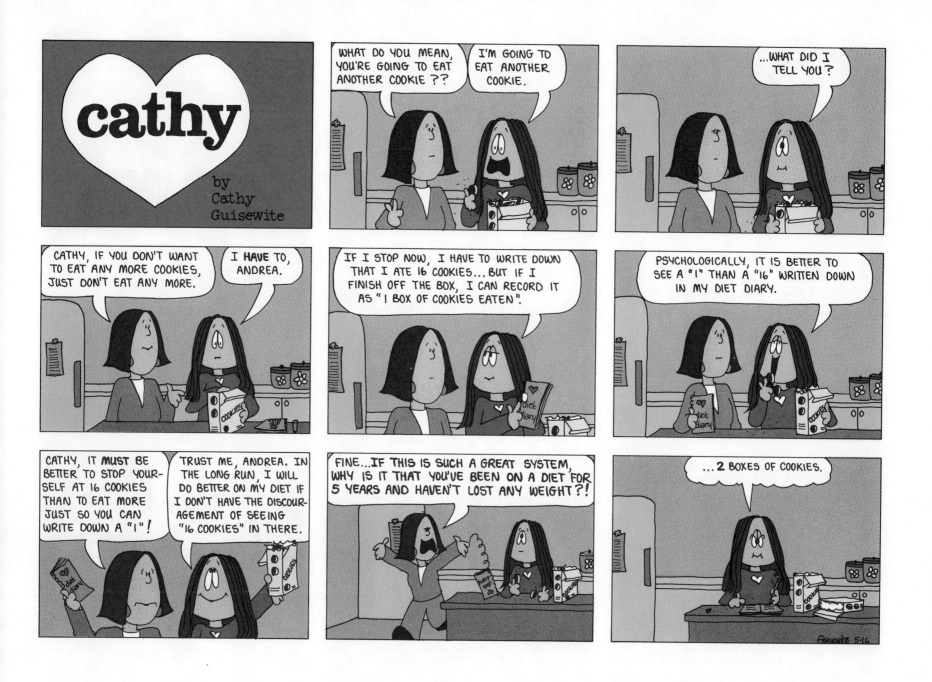

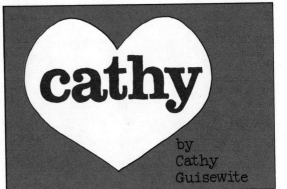

cathy

by Cathy Guisewite

THERE'S A U-HAUL IN FRONT OF YOUR APARTMENT BUILDING AGAIN, CATHY.

JOE AND ELLEN MUST HAVE HAD ANOTHER FIGHT.

ELLEN LOST.

WHEN A WOMAN DUMPS A MAN, SHE GIVES HIM EVERYTHING....WHY? SHE FEELS GUILTY.

WHEN A MAN DUMPS A WOMAN, THE WOMAN **STILL** GIVES HIM EVERYTHING.....WHY? SHE WANTS TO GET HIM BACK.

SHOW ME A MAN WHO'S BEEN THROUGH A LOT OF RELATIONSHIPS ...AND I'LL SHOW YOU A MAN WITH AN APARTMENT FULL OF FURNITURE!!

THAT'S A VERY UNFAIR GENERALIZATION.

CATHY, IT'S TRUE. WOMEN ARE SO CONDITIONED TO GIVING THAT EVEN WHEN THEY CAN'T STAND A GUY ANYMORE, THEY WIND UP GIVING HIM THE LIVING ROOM SOFA!

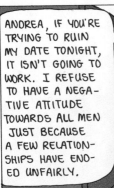

ANDREA, IF YOU'RE TRYING TO RUIN MY DATE TONIGHT, IT ISN'T GOING TO WORK. I REFUSE TO HAVE A NEGATIVE ATTITUDE TOWARDS ALL MEN JUST BECAUSE A FEW RELATIONSHIPS HAVE ENDED UNFAIRLY.

SO...WHAT DO YOU THINK OF MY PLACE?

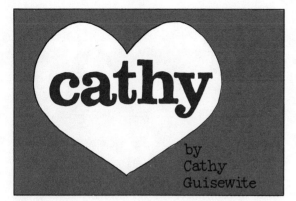

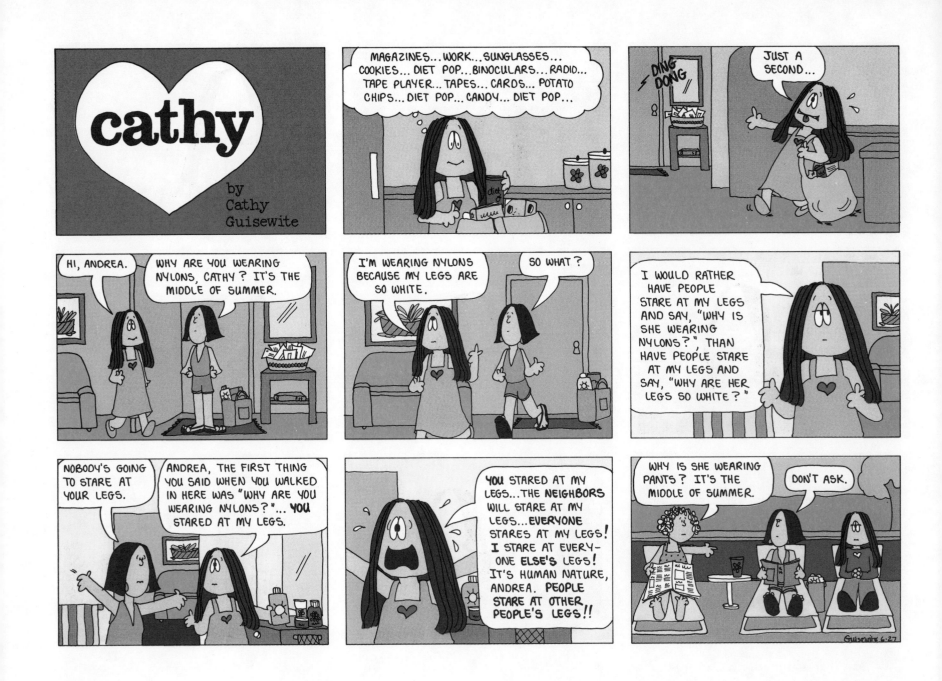

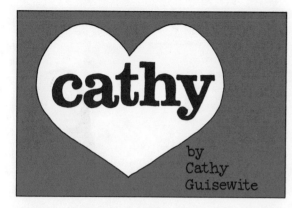

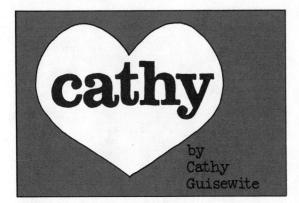

cathy

by
Cathy
Guisewite

DO YOU HAVE A DATE FOR THE FOURTH OF JULY, CATHY?

I'M WORKING ON IT.

HADN'T YOU BETTER HURRY UP?

REMEMBER WHEN WE WERE IN HIGH SCHOOL AND WE USED TO THINK, "IF I CONCENTRATE REALLY HARD, I WILL BE ABLE TO FIGURE OUT WHERE THIS CERTAIN GUY IS AND WILL THEN MAGICALLY RUN INTO HIM JUST WHEN I'M LOOKING PARTICULARLY CUTE"?

YEAH. HOO, BOY!! WERE WE YOUNG!!

I STILL DO THAT.

WHAT DO YOU MEAN, YOU STILL DO THAT??

I DIDN'T THINK I DID, ANDREA, BUT I MET SOMEONE NEW AND I FIND I'M STILL DOING THAT.

CATHY, THAT'S **DISGUSTING**! THAT'S EVEN WORSE THAN WHEN WE USED TO SIT AROUND AT NIGHT TRYING TO CONTACT SOME GUY THROUGH E.S.P. TO GET HIM TO CALL!!

AHEM...

YAAA!! YOU STILL DO THAT TOO!!!

CONFESSION CLEANSES THE SOUL, BUT MESSES UP THE KITCHEN.

Guisewite 7-4

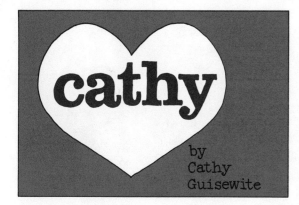

cathy

by Cathy Guisewite

IS THAT MY PHONE RINGING?

THERE IS NO PHONE RINGING.

HOW DO YOU KNOW?

TRUST ME...

WE MADE THAT PRESENTATION TO THE BRAX COMPANY A WEEK AGO. WHY DON'T THEY CALL AND TELL US WHERE WE STAND?

BECAUSE THEY'RE MEN, MR. PINKLEY.

MEN ONLY CALL WHEN YOU DON'T CARE ANYMORE. WHY SHOULD THEY ACT ANY DIFFERENTLY IN BUSINESS?

MEN FIGURE OUT YOUR CRACKING POINT, WAIT TWO DAYS, AND THEN CALL AND SAY, "HI! WHAT'S NEW?"

YOU WANT THE GUYS AT THE BRAX COMPANY TO CALL?... EAT A BOX OF DONUTS, RIP UP ALL THEIR LETTERS, AND SCREAM AT THE TOP OF YOUR LUNGS, I NEVER WANT TO SEE YOUR MISERABLE FACES AGAIN!!

...WANT THEM TO PAY YOU A VISIT? INVITE THEIR COMPETITION OVER, SO IT WOULD BE THE WORST POSSIBLE MOMENT FOR THEM TO SHOW UP AND...VOILÁ! ENTER THE BRAX BOYS!!

IS THERE SOMETHING YOU WANT TO TALK ABOUT, CATHY?

YOU KNOW I NEVER BRING MY PERSONAL PROBLEMS TO THE OFFICE, MR. PINKLEY.

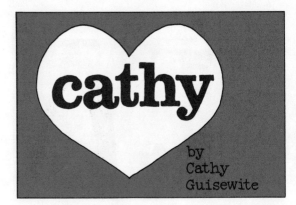

cathy

by Cathy Guisewite

IRVING IS SO HANDSOME. IRVING IS SO CHARMING. IRVING IS SO SWEET. ISN'T HE?

WHAT DO YOU WANT ME TO SAY?

GUESS.

ARE YOU SUDDENLY STARTING TO SAY HOW MUCH YOU LIKE IRVING BECAUSE YOU WANT ME TO LIKE HIM, CATHY?

WHAT ARE YOU TALKING ABOUT, MOM?

OR ARE YOU DOING THIS BECAUSE YOU THINK I'LL DO THE OPPOSITE OF WHAT YOU SAY AND YOU WANT ME TO NOT LIKE HIM?

MAYBE YOU'VE DECIDED YOU DON'T LIKE HIM, BUT YOU'RE SAYING YOU DO LIKE HIM SO I'LL SAY I DON'T LIKE HIM AND THEN WE CAN AGREE WITH EACH OTHER WITHOUT ACTUALLY HAVING TO ADMIT IT.

OR DO YOU THINK I'LL KNOW YOU'RE TRYING REVERSE PSYCHOLOGY SO INSTEAD OF NOT LIKING HIM, I'LL WIND UP LIKING HIM? OR ARE YOU TRYING TO GET ME SO CONFUSED I WON'T BE ABLE TO FORM AN OPINION?

THERE'S NOTHING WORSE THAN UNDERSTANDING YOUR CHILDREN.

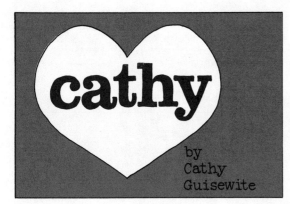

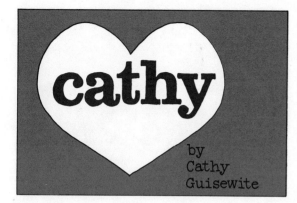

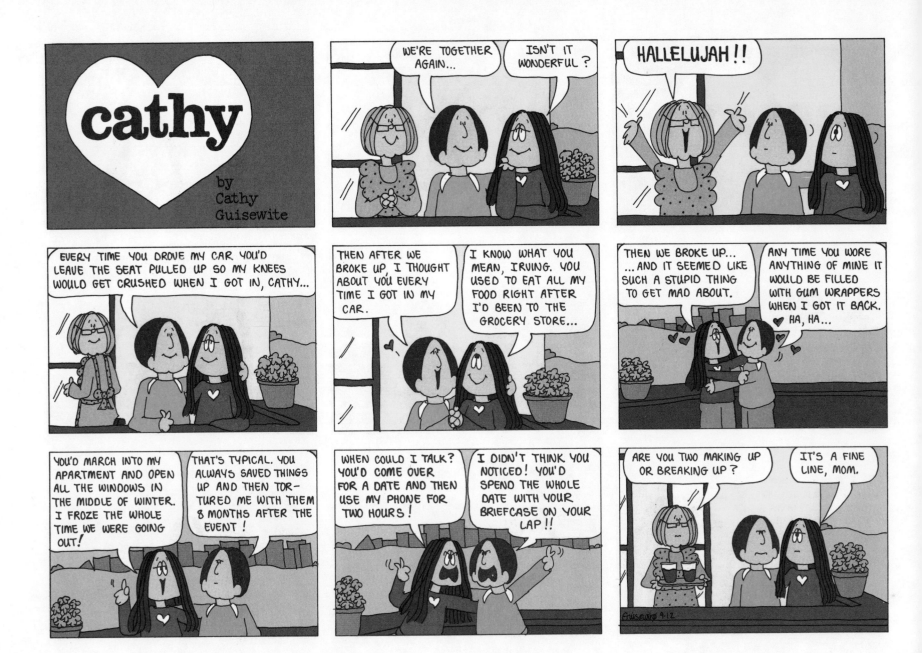

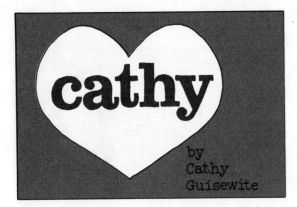

cathy

by Cathy Guisewite

WHERE'S MABEL?

SHE'S HIDING IN THE EMPLOYEE LOUNGE.

TELL HER SHE HAS A CUSTOMER.

WHY DO YOU THINK SHE'S HIDING?

HELLO, MABEL. I WANT MY MONEY BACK FOR THIS SUIT.

YOU MUST BE JOKING. YOU BOUGHT THAT LAST YEAR.

WHEN YOU TALKED ME INTO PAYING $200 FOR THIS SUIT, YOU SAID IT WAS A "CLASSIC LOOK". "AN INVESTMENT", YOU SAID. "THESE TAILORED SERIOUS LINES WILL NEVER GO OUT OF STYLE!"

THEY WENT OUT OF STYLE IN SIX MONTHS, MABEL.

OOPS! WELL, MAYBE YOU'RE JUST NOT USING YOUR IMAGINATION.

HERE... SIMPLY GET SOME DAINTY PUMPS... A FRILLY BLOUSE... A WIDE SUEDE BELT... AND HAVE THE JACKET AND SKIRT RE-TAILORED! FOR $200 YOU COULD MAKE THIS A BRAND NEW OUTFIT!

IF I HAD $200, I WOULDN'T BE WORRYING ABOUT REVIVING LAST YEAR'S SUIT!!

OH, BUT IT'S WORTH IT! IT WOULD BE SUCH A CLASSIC LOOK ... AN INVESTMENT...

...THESE SOFT, FEMININE LINES WILL NEVER GO OUT OF STYLE!

10-10

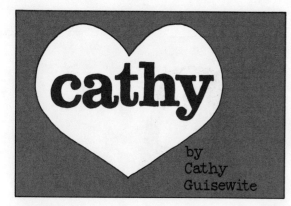

cathy

by
Cathy
Guisewite

ARE YOU SURE EVERYONE ELSE WILL BE WEARING COSTUMES, ANDREA?

OF COURSE EVERYONE WILL BE WEARING COSTUMES.

KNOCK KNOCK

HI. GLAD YOU COULD COME.

YOU TOLD ME THIS WAS A COSTUME PARTY, ANDREA.

YOU **SWORE** EVERYONE WOULD BE WEARING COSTUMES.

WHAT ARE YOU TALKING ABOUT, CATHY? EVERYONE HERE IS WEARING A COSTUME.

CAROL IS DRESSED AS AN UNDERPAID SECRETARY WHO SPENT HER RENT MONEY ON ONE GOOD DRESS... JOAN CAME AS A 60's RADICAL-GONE-GUCCI...PAM REPRESENTS THE ETERNAL CONFLICT BETWEEN PEASANT AND PUNK...

THE MEN ALL CAME AS EXECUTIVES ON THE VERGE OF A LAY-OFF, AND I, OF COURSE, AM THE ESSENCE OF AUTUMN IN THE SHAPE OF A WOMAN.

BELIEVE ME, CATHY, WE ALL FEEL RIDICULOUS AT THESE THINGS!

HOW COMFORTING.

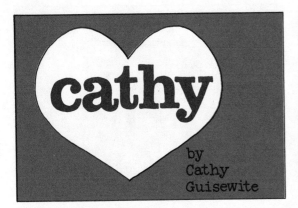

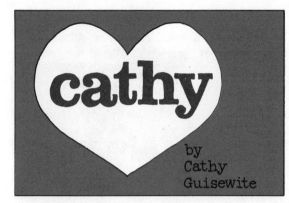

cathy

by Cathy Guisewite

CAN YOU GET THE DOOR, ANDREA?

WITH WHAT?

LOOK AT ALL THIS!

MY BUDGET. MY 2-WEEK MENU PLAN. MY SHOPPING LIST. MY GROCERIES. MY RECEIPT.

I HATE TO ADMIT IT, ANDREA, BUT MY MOTHER WAS RIGHT. SHOPPING THIS WAY IS GOING TO CHANGE MY LIFE!

I HAVE TWO SOLID WEEKS OF NUTRITIOUS MEALS HERE, FOR A FRACTION OF WHAT THE JUNK FOOD I USUALLY EAT WOULD HAVE COST!

IT'S SO EASY, ANDREA! JUST A LITTLE PLANNING AND...

HI, CATHY. WHAT DID YOU BUY??

WANT TO GO OUT FOR A CHEESEBURGER?

CAN I BORROW A DOLLAR?

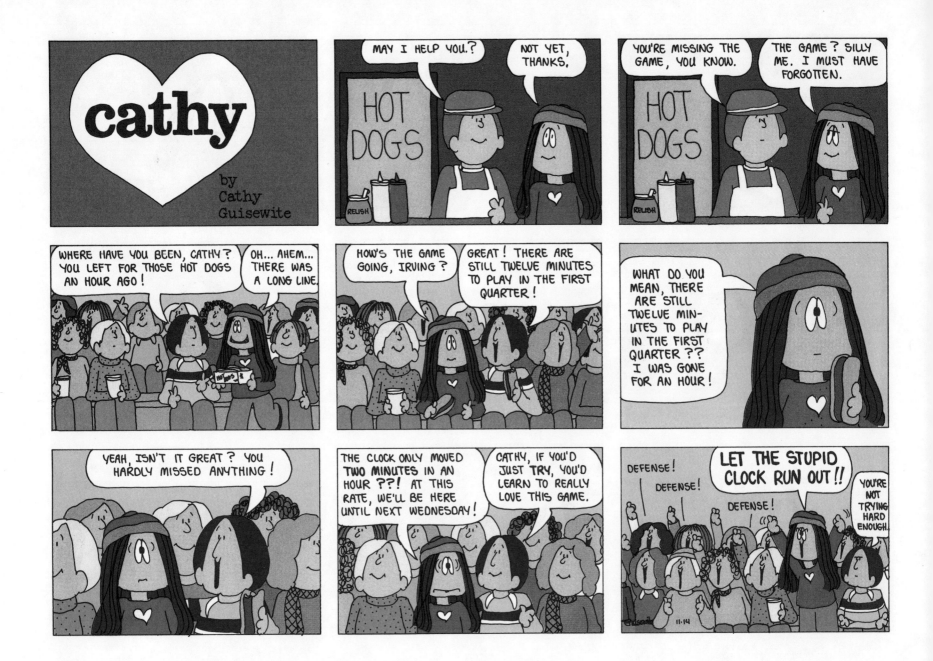

cathy
by Cathy Guisewite

JUST A SECOND, IRVING. I'M A LITTLE...

LATE.

NOW I'M... ANNOYED.

IRVING, I'M...

I KNOW, CATHY. YOU'RE FREEZING. FROM NOW UNTIL THE FOURTH OF JULY, YOU'LL BE FREEZING.

APARTMENTS 299-399

...EXCEPT FOR WHEN YOU GO CHRISTMAS SHOPPING WITH YOUR COAT ON. THEN YOU'LL BE BOILING.

IN BETWEEN FREEZING AND BOILING, YOU'LL GO ON A SERIES OF HOLIDAY CRASH DIETS. YOU'LL BE STARVING.

YOU'LL GO **OFF** THE DIETS. YOU'LL BE STUFFED.

YOU WON'T BE ABLE TO FIND THE GIFTS YOU WANT. YOU'LL BE FRUSTRATED. YOU'LL SPEND ALL YOUR MONEY ANYWAY. YOU'LL BE BROKE. CHRISTMAS WILL COME. YOU'LL BE HAPPY. THEN IT WILL BE NEW YEAR'S AND YOU'LL BE A LUNATIC FOR 6 MONTHS BECAUSE YOU'RE BREAKING ALL YOUR RESOLUTIONS!!

HE ANTICIPATES MY EVERY MOOD.

12·5

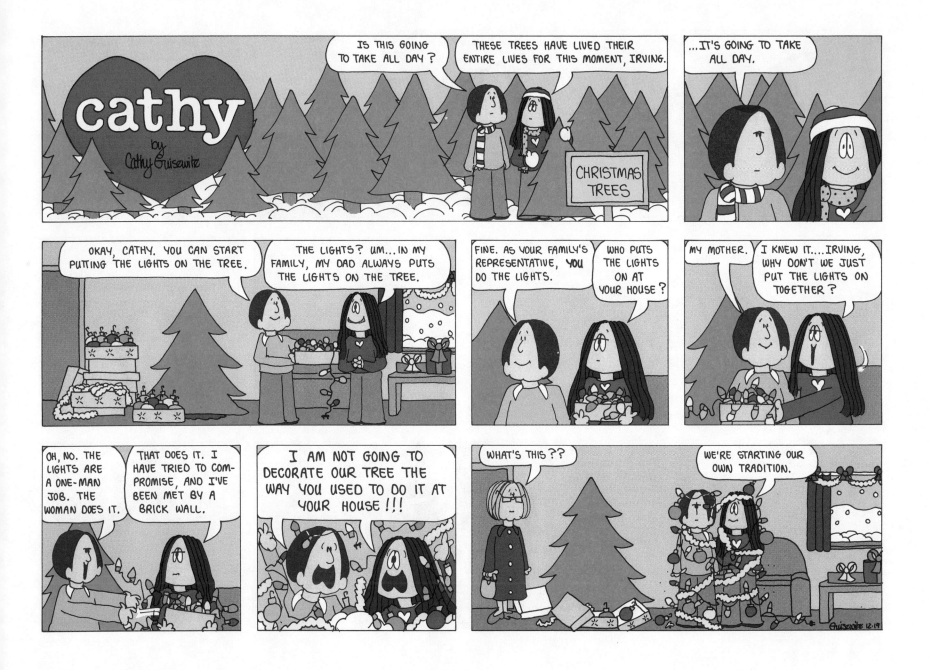

...SO AUNT LOUISE'S THIRD HUSBAND SAID...

YOUR AUNT HAD THREE HUSBANDS??

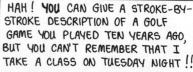

YOU DIDN'T REMEMBER MY AUNT LOUISE HAD THREE HUSBANDS??

I DIDN'T EVEN REMEMBER YOU HAD AN AUNT LOUISE.

CATHY, HOW IS IT THAT YOU'VE FORGOTTEN EVERYTHING I'VE TOLD YOU ABOUT MY FAMILY, BUT YOU CAN GIVE ME AN EXACT REPLAY OF AN ARGUMENT WE HAD THREE YEARS AGO??

IRVING, **YOU** CAN REMEMBER THE PLAYERS, TEAMS AND SCORES OF 300 FOOTBALL GAMES, BUT YOU CAN'T REMEMBER MY BIRTHDAY.

OH YEAH? WELL, **YOU** CAN REMEMBER EVERY SINGLE TIME I WAS LATE FOR A DATE, BUT YOU CAN'T REMEMBER WHAT KIND OF OIL YOUR OWN CAR TAKES!!

HAH! **YOU** CAN GIVE A STROKE-BY-STROKE DESCRIPTION OF A GOLF GAME YOU PLAYED TEN YEARS AGO, BUT YOU CAN'T REMEMBER THAT I TAKE A CLASS ON TUESDAY NIGHT!!

OH YEAH?? WELL **YOU**...

...YOU, UM.. AHEM..

AHEM...UM..

THIS IS STUPID, ISN'T IT?

YEAH...LET'S SEE WHAT'S ON TV.

WHAT HAPPENED TO YOUR FIGHT?

WE BOTH RAN OUT OF AMMUNITION AT THE SAME TIME.

Guisewite 8-13

cathy

by Cathy Guisewite

☼ THE ORGANIC GROCER ☼

* NO PRESERVATIVES
* NO ADDITIVES
* NO ARTIFICIAL FLAVORING
* NO ARTIFICIAL COLORING

* NO CHECKS

NATURE'S HEARTH BLUEBERRY MUFFINS...

WHOLE WHEAT PECAN-YOGURT WAFFLE MIX... ORGANICALLY HARVESTED MAPLE SYRUP... SESAME HERB CRACKERS... WALNUT-RAISIN GRANOLA... 7-GRAIN PROTEIN COOKIES...

YOGURT COATED ALMONDS... CAROB MALT BALLS... PEANUT-CASHEW CHEW...

WHOLE WHEAT FIG BARS... HONEY-NUT PROTEIN CRUNCH... BANANA CHIP TRAIL MIX...

STONE GROUND TAMARI CORN CHIPS... SUNFLOWER SEED CARROT CAKE... CAROB-NUT BROWNIES... EARTH SPROUTED ZUCCHINI LASAGNA...

CAROB-HONEY ICE CREAM... PEANUT BUTTER PROTEIN SHAKE... ORGANIC WHOLE WHEAT PIZZA...

CRUNCH CHEW CHEW

...THIS DIET DIED OF NATURAL CAUSES.

3-20 Guisewite

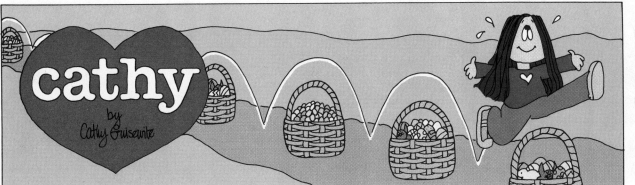

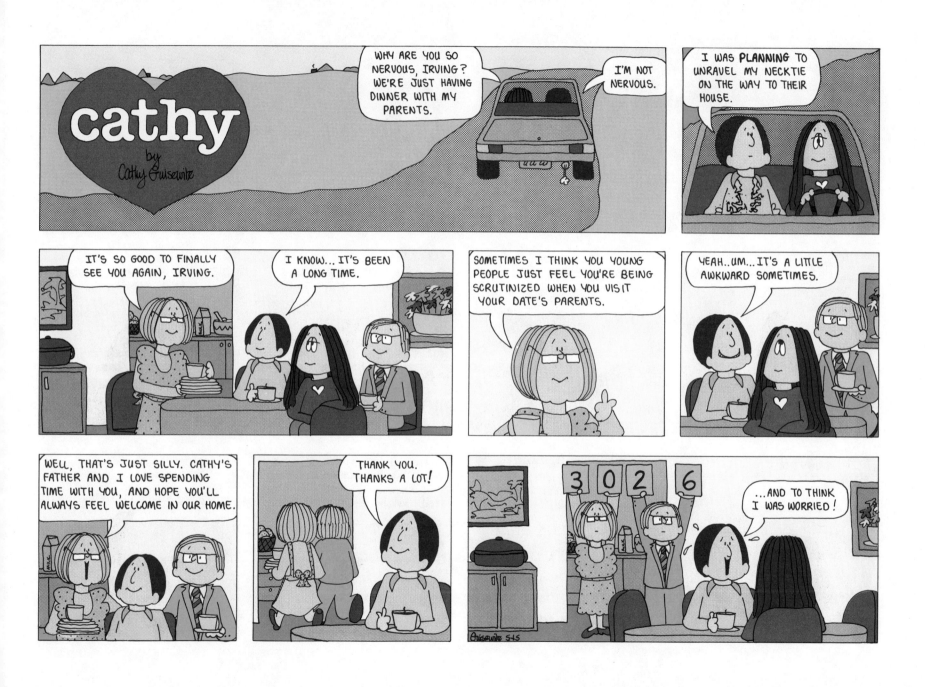

HAPPY FATHER'S DAY!

cathy
by Cathy Guisewite

WILL EIGHT CHICKEN LEGS EACH BE ENOUGH?

GEE, I DON'T KNOW...CATHY, WHAT DO YOU THINK?

DEPENDS ON WHAT ELSE WE'RE HAVING.

HAVE A NICE FATHER'S DAY PICNIC, AND REMEMBER...

..."BRING HOME THE ALUMINUM FOIL."

YOUR MOTHER'S BEEN USING THIS SAME PIECE OF ALUMINUM FOIL SINCE 1953, CATHY.

DOESN'T IT MAKE YOU NUTS, DAD?

I DON'T MIND THE FOIL SO MUCH...IT'S THE PLASTIC SPOONS. IN 30 YEARS OF MARRIAGE, SHE'S NEVER THROWN AWAY A PLASTIC SPOON!

I KNOW. I WATCHED HER SPEND $95.00 ON DRAWER ORGANIZERS SO HER 2,700 USED TWIST-TIES WOULDN'T GET MIXED IN WITH HER 4,500 RE-USABLE COFFEE STIRRERS!

I TRIED TO SNEAK OUT WITH HER COLLECTION OF EMPTY JUICE CANS ONCE...SHE CHASED ME BACK INTO THE HOUSE WITH HER 25-YEAR-OLD RECONSTRUCTED BROOM!!

HOW DO YOU STAND IT?

ACTUALLY, IT'S KIND OF NICE. A WOMAN WHO'S SAVED THE LITTLE PLASTIC HANGER FROM EVERY PAIR OF MY SOCKS IS HARDLY GOING TO DECIDE TO DUMP ME!

AAACK! DON'T THROW OUT THE DISPOSABLE SALT SHAKERS!

OOPS. I FORGOT..."THOSE LITTLE DISPOSABLE SALT SHAKERS WILL MAKE WONDERFUL TOYS IF THERE ARE EVER ANY GRANDCHILDREN!!"

WELL, IT SOUNDS LIKE YOU TWO HAD FUN! WHAT DID YOU TALK ABOUT ALL DAY?

THE OFFICE.

Guisewite 6-19

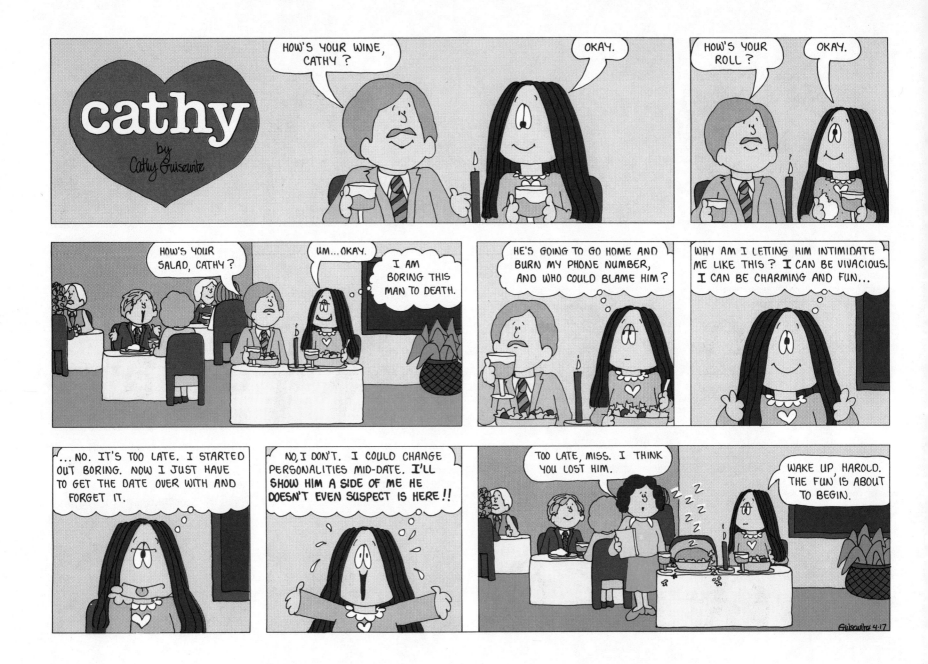